For Oona and Anita, the bravest girls in the bath —SR

For Elijah and Marissa, who are so wonderful it's scary —TT

About This Book
The illustrations for this book were rendered digitally. This book was edited by Farrin Jacobs and designed by Karina Granda. The production was supervised by Bernadette Flinn, and the production editor was Jen Graham. The text was set in Adobe Garamond Pro, and the display type is Bodoni Antiqua Compressed.

Little, Brown and Company
Hachette Book Group
1290 Avenue of the Americas, New York, NY 10104
Visit us at LBYR.com

First Edition: April 2022

Little, Brown and Company is a division of Hachette Book Group, Inc.
The Little, Brown name and logo are trademarks of Hachette Book Group, Inc.

The publisher is not responsible for websites (or their content) that are not owned by the publisher.

Library of Congress Cataloging-in-Publication Data
Names: Rich, Simon, author. | Toro, Tom, illustrator.
Title: I'm terrified of bath time / by Simon Rich ; illustrated by Tom Toro. Other titles: I am terrified of bath time
Description: First edition. | New York : Little, Brown and Company, 2022. | Summary: A bathtub, who is just as terrified of bath time as the little girl who bathes in him, offers suggestions on how to make the experience better for both of them.
Identifiers: LCCN 2020029700 | ISBN 9780316628334 (hardcover)
Subjects: CYAC: Baths—Fiction. | Fear—Fiction. | Bathtubs—Fiction.
Classification: LCC PZ7.1.R5323 Im 2022 | DDC [E]—dc23
LC record available at https://lccn.loc.gov/2020029700

ISBN 978-0-316-62833-4

PRINTED IN CHINA

APS

10 9 8 7 6 5 4 3 2 1

I'M TERRIFIED OF BATH TIME

Can I tell you a secret?

I'm terrified of bath time.

Usually, being a bathtub is fun. I just hang out all day with my friends Sink and Toilet.

But then, each night, I hear those dreaded words …

And the fear sets in.

It's the same every time.
First, a scary giant comes into my room.

Then he twists my eyeballs.

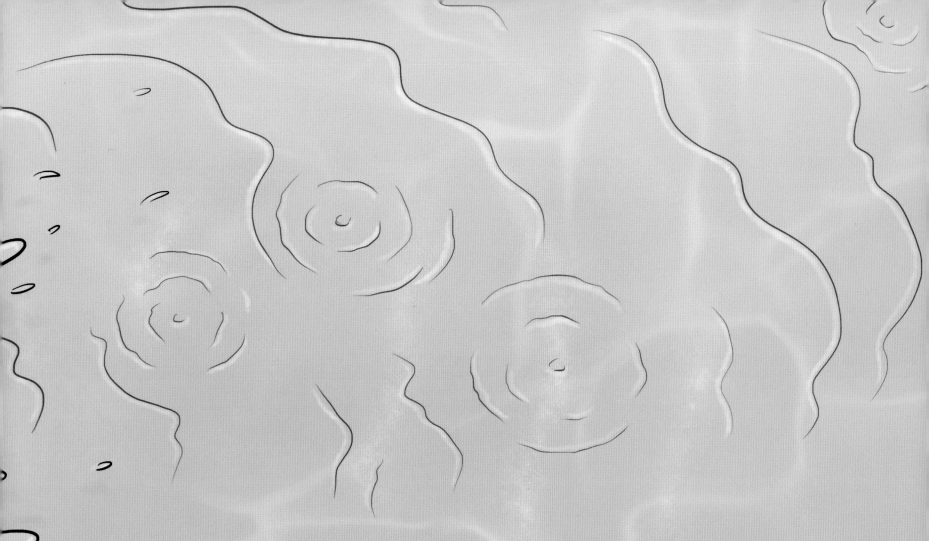

I get so freaked out I shoot water out my nose.
You would not believe how weird it feels.

I look to Sink and Toilet for support,
but those two are no help.

When I'm full of water, I really start to panic.

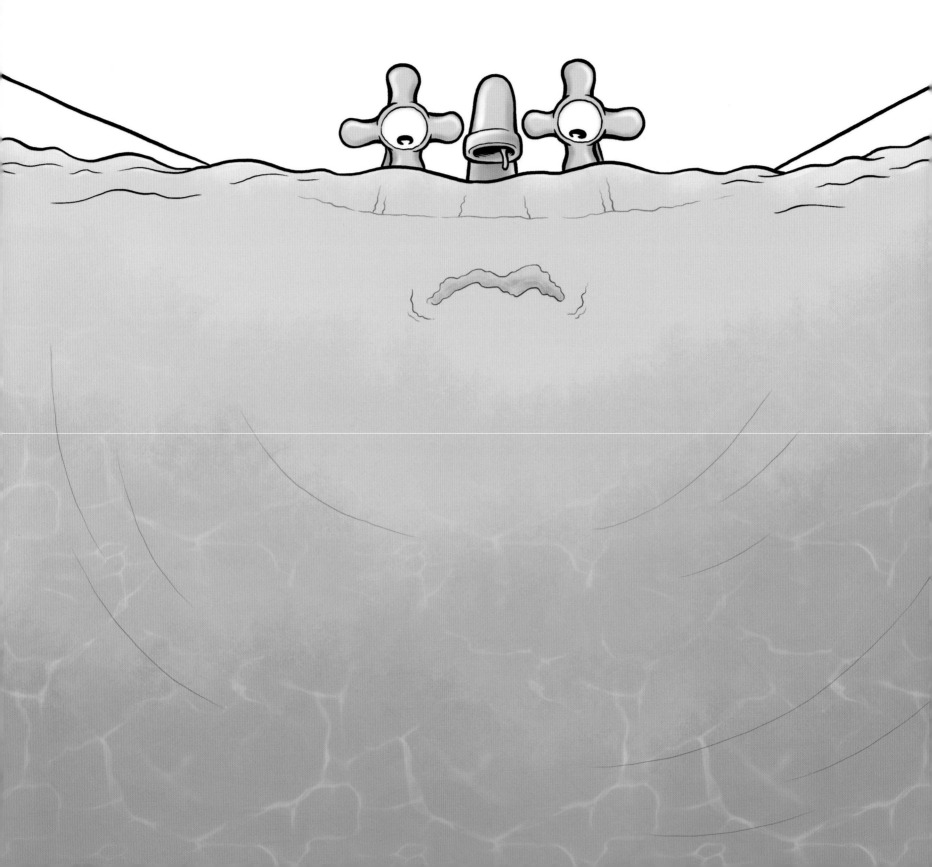

Because I know what's coming next …

You.

Listen. I know you've got your own issues with bath time. But compared to me, you've got it easy.

You can splash.

You can flail.

All I can do is try to survive.

Sometimes you kick my nose.

Sometimes you scream in my ear.

One time you pooped.

That was a low point for us both.

The fact is:

You have all the power in this relationship.

Which is why I'm asking for a favor.

Tonight, please have mercy on me.
Tonight, please be kind.

Instead of screaming in my ear, try singing me a song.
I love songs!

Instead of kicking my nose, try giving me a makeover.
I'm overdue!

Instead of pooping...
Well, to be honest, pretty much anything
would be an improvement over that.

Bath time doesn't have to be scary. With your help,
I bet we can even make it sort of fun.

We'll have such a good time,
we'll make Sink and Toilet jealous.

And I'll be so happy, I'll shoot water out my nose.

It will still feel weird.

But in a good way.